I LOST MY MIND

A fiction yet factual book series to help overcome the maze of the mind.

Mission: To Proclaim Transformation and Truth
Publisher: Transformed Publishing, Cocoa, FL
Website: www.transformedpublishing.com
Email: transformedpublishing@gmail.com

© Copyright 2022 by Diana Robinson

Cover Design: Grace Glace lilyvalleymktg@gmail.com

All rights reserved solely by the author. No part of this book may be reproduced, stored in a retrieval system, or transmitted in any form or by any means without expressed written permission of the author.

This is a work of fiction and not a recommended course of treatment for any mentioned life issues (relational, medical, mental, emotional, substance abuse, etc.). Names, characters, organizations, places, events, and incidents are either products of the author's imagination or are used fictitiously.

Scriptures are taken from the New King James Version ®. Copyright © 1982 by Thomas Nelson. Used by permission. All rights reserved.

Bible page excerpt on pg. 33 was taken from author's personal copy of The Holy Bible Copyright © 1992 by Thomas Nelson, Inc. page 1341 & 1342.

ISBN: 978-1-953241-35-1

I LOST MY MIND

TIED, DESTROYED, TORMENTED, & CONFUSED

Diana Robinson

TABLE OF CONTENTS

1: Tye Ied...................1
2: Dee Stroyed............4
3: Tye & Dee................7
4: Torie Mented..........9
5: Conner Fused........11
6: Wake Up, Torie!.13
7: Car Rider..............16
8: Happy Hour........19
9: Takeout..................21
10: Text-to-Text.........24
11: Night -Night........27
12: Time Crunch..........29
13: Game Day............35
14: Knock Knock.......39
15: Concession Stand..41
16: I'm Ready...........44
17: Mommy, Me, & Little Mes.............48
18: Kick Off..............51
19: Saturday Night Decisions...............56
20: Pancakes!..............58
21: Rise & Fall...........61
22: Church..................63
23: Virtual..................66
24: Coincidence or Purposeful.............72
25: Home Sweet Home.....................77
26: Around the Corner....................79
27: Thank You...........82
28: Monday Morning...............86
29: Lunch is Served....88
30: Dinner Plans.......91

About the Author..........96

More Transformed Publishing Books.........97

Friday Morning

1

Tye Iced

No!
Hell no!
I'm not going.
It's all a bunch of bullshit anyway.

Tye asked politely, "What time did you say?"

"11 a.m. every Sunday," Steven responded expecting another excuse.

"I finally got my kids this weekend. I haven't seen them much. I don't want to have to drag 'em out of bed early on a Sunday morning," Tye explained.

"Your kids sleep til 11 a.m. on the weekends? Now, that is unheard of. We actually have a field day and BBQ after church this Sunday. During children's church, all the kids will be practicing a special song to perform during the event."

I LOST MY MIND

Damn, I just don't want to go. Shut up already. I don't even know how my kids would act at a church. Tell yourself the truth Tye, you don't know how they act anywhere because you barely see them.

Wrestling with his own thoughts, Tye realized Steven was still talking to him.

"Tye, I thought your daughter loves to sing and your sons are natural born athletes. They would have a great time." Steven noticed Tye's hesitation and decided to end the conversation, "I'm going to text you the flyer, so you have the information. I gotta get in my office to prep for my 8:30 virtual meeting."

Tye watched Steven walk down the hall in his button up shirt, tie, slacks, and flip-flops, carrying his lunchbox packed by his wife.

It must be nice.

Entering his own office, Tye threw his snack bag full of random convenience store items on the shelf and opened his laptop. Time to check his bank account. This is one of the few months of the year there are three pay weeks. No healthcare premiums come out of his paycheck on this rare occasion and no child support garnishments.

I might actually have a comma in my paycheck today! Carrying the kids on my health insurance is more than my car payment every month. The amount of child support I pay is twenty dollars less than my rent. The youngest will be eighteen in seven more years. Come on lucky seven!

After spinning for about thirty seconds, Tye's bank account information loaded on the screen.

Yes! Freedom! Damn! That check looks right! Maybe they pay me better than I realized. I don't know how so many other guys get out of paying child support. I can't take no chances. No jail for me.

2

Dee Strayed

I'll be so glad to have the kids out of the house this weekend. They are always watching everything I do. Like get off my ass – I'm grown.

"Did you all pack enough draws? Two nights you will be gone, so you at least need three pairs. And get your lunch money from ya daddy for the whole week on Sunday night," Dee yelled down the hall while scrolling through social media.

Baby girl came to Dee's door and asked, "Mom, what do we need to bring? What are we going to be doing each day?"

How the hell am I supposed to know what your missing in action father got planned? Fix your face. Dee, answer nice. You are about to drop these kids off at school and live your best life all the way until Sunday night.

*Friday,
Saturday,
Sunday.*

Girl, you deserve it!

"Baby girl, I'm not sure what your daddy has planned, but I know it's gonna be great," Dee responded contrary to her thoughts.

"Last time we went over there he wouldn't even let us go down to the pool," baby girl protested.

"Probably because it was too cold outside. The weather is good now. Pack your bathing suit and goggles. Now, hurry up so you are not late for school."

*Look at that ol' bullshit!
Ol' asshole hasn't had the kids
over since it was cold outside.
And here we are –
been sweating at least a month now.*

"I'm getting in the car. I need all of you loaded up in the next three minutes or I'm pulling off without you," Dee hollered as she balanced her coffee, purse, laptop, cell phone, and her own overnight bag.

I love you all, but I need me some 'me time'!

I LOST MY MIND

Dee got into the car, texted her boyfriend back and forth a few times, then started honking the horn.

Shit, that horn is too loud up in this garage.

Dee popped the trunk once the kids started exiting the house and poked her head out of the window, "Stick your bags in the trunk. We should have pulled out of this driveway three minutes ago to get you all to school on time."

3

Tye & Dee

> Just dropped the kids off at school.
> Tag, you're it!
> I'm off the grid til Sunday night.
> Figure it out.

8:23 a.m. Dee

> And make sure you give them enough lunch money for the whole week when you drop them off. My money hasn't been like I need it to be these last few months.

8:24 a.m. Dee

Trippin'
Tye – don't trip back.
She is trynna get to you.

I LOST MY MIND

She can work 20 hours a week and bring home more money than you do after working a 60-hour week. Why? Because nearly half of what YOU make is direct deposited into HER account!

> Will do.
> Enjoy.
>
> **8:26 a.m.**   **$$$ TYE $$$**

Oh, yeah!
I'm gonna enjoy - you ol' sorry ass!
I have a lot to enjoy this weekend.

> You too. The kids are looking forward to seeing you.
>
> **8:28 a.m.**   **Dee** ♥

And I'm sure you're looking forward to a whole bunch of alcohol, dancing, and talkin' shit with your homegirls.

> I'm excited to see them too.
>
> **8:29 a.m.**   **$$$ TYE $$$**

4

Torie Mented

Get up.
Get UP.
GET UP!
Why is it so hard for me to face every day?

"The alarm went off three times. I'm just checking on you Mrs. Torie to make sure you are feeling alright," Allie said from the doorway.

"I'm not a child. I can take care of myself. Close my door please and give your attention back to the kids," Torie scolded.

I LOST MY MIND

Blindly reaching around in the top draw of her nightstand, Torie groped for her pills. The *daytime* pills, to get her out of bed, since the *nighttime* ones did such a good job of knocking her out. Unable to secure a grip on her pill bottle, Torie took notice of the time on her digital clock, then decided to roll over to go back to sleep.

Nine months old and almost three years old, Torie silently listened to her daughters laughing as they started their day.

How can you all be so happy coming from such a miserable mother?

5

Conner Fused

Decisions,
     decisions,
          decisions.
I'm five years passed the coveted milestone age of eighteen and still don't have a clue.

"So, which degree track would you like to pursue?" Ms. Matthews kindly asked again.

Ms. Matthews has been more than patient. I know she probably wanted to say, "Which degree track would you like to pursue now you indecisive silver spoon fed millennial?"

"You have a lot of credits. It is important to commit to a specific program so you can obtain your degree. Conner, you have worked hard. Your grades are stellar. Your leadership roles on campus are highly esteemed. You

I LOST MY MIND

obviously can do anything you put your mind to and do *it* better than most people. You have taken a range of electives. What piques your interest? What do you see yourself doing long term?"

> *I don't know. That is my problem. What if I make the wrong choice? I would let down so many people who have invested in my education and been such an integral part of my upbringing.*

"What do you recommend, Ms. Matthews?"
"No, Conner. I can't make this decision for you. Every semester for the last five years, we have sat down and made a *different* plan. I'm an advisor and I advise you to *FOCUS* - Follow One Course Until Success."

"Now, that is a great acronym, Ms. Matthews. Did you make that up yourself?"

"No. My pastor said it at church."

Conner asked surprisingly, "Your pastor teaches about success in life?"

"Yes, we are heaven bound, but must live heaven on earth until we get there."

"I'm going to come back next week with my final-final selection. As always, thank you for your time."

Conner walked down the steps instead of taking the elevator. Once he was alone, he said out loud to himself, "Follow One Course Until Success."

Friday Afternoon

6

Wake Up, Torie!

12:15?
Noon or midnight?
What has happened to me?
I used to have my life together.

Giggling and ABC's. Okay. It's still daytime.
Kids sound good. Allie is doing her thing.
I'm glad the kids have her.
Nanny extraordinaire.

Get up Torie. Get up!

I LOST MY MIND

Serious about actually getting out of bed, Torie sat up and turned on her bedside lamp. The blackout curtains really worked. It was dark in the room and darker in her heart and mind.

Why? Why? Why?
How could God give us two beautiful
children and then kill my husband?
He did everything right.
Everything. Everything.
Everything right.

Two and a half years with our first daughter and
six months with our second. The perfect father.
Ten years married. The perfect husband.
Faithful.
Gone.

Get up Torie. Get up!

Taking the cap off of her water, Torie placed the open bottle on her nightstand and located her *get up & function* pill bottle.

I definitely need a double dose today.
Double-Double!
I at least want to be able to take the kids out back
on the swing set and let Allie get out of the house
for a few hours. Yes, that is today's goal.
Shower.
Swing set.

Throwing her head back, Torie swallowed her medication, and drank half her bottle of water. Tears streamed down her face.

I gotta take that picture down.
I can't take that picture down.
Look away, Torie.
Get up.
Get in the shower.
Shower.
Swing set.

7

Car Rider

How do people wait in this long ass line every day? This is ridiculous.
I still gotta pick up the older two from the football field. Seems like paying child support may be worth it after all – to buy my way out of this traffic jam...

"Who are you here to pick up, sir?"
"My daughter, Dominique Ied."
"What grade is she in, sir? You really should have a car rider name plate in your window."
"Sixth grade. Her mother usually picks her up?"
"Are you even on her pickup list, sir? Maybe you should park."

Park? I have been parked in this so-called pickup line for thirty-three minutes now.

"There she is, right there," Tye said pointing, "Dominique, let's go baby girl."

"Sir, you are going to have to park and come in so we can make sure you are on her pickup list. Please bring your ID in with you."

"What? I am her father. Ask her! She will tell you," Tye rebutted, "Dominique, come on!"

"He is. That is her father Ms. Prescot. He is authorized to pick up Dominique. Come on Dominique, let's get you in the car," Ms. Addilyn, Dominique's fourth grade teacher, said as she waved to her to approach the car. "Good to see you again, Mr. Ied. Dominique is impressing her sixth-grade teachers with the higher-level Math she is doing," Ms. Addilyn closed the car door once Dominique was inside and wished them a good weekend.

Driving off, Tye could see that Dominique was upset, probably embarrassed, so he tried to *break the ice*.

"Good to see you baby girl! That sure is a safe and secure school you go to."

"Daddy, that was so embarrassing. I have been in the same school since kindergarten, and no one recognized your face. What does that tell you?"

"That is not true. Ms. Angel recognized me."

"Ms. Addilyn, Daddy! And that is because Mom always said she thought that lady had a crush on you."

"Can you blame her?"

"Let's change the subject please, Daddy. What are we doing this weekend?"

I LOST MY MIND

"It's still up in the air. We got to talk about it."

"So, you didn't plan anything?"

"Right now, we are picking up your brothers from the football field and then going to get some takeout for dinner."

"Oh wow, so we won't be home for at least another hour. Can I watch my show on your phone, Daddy? Please."

"Grab it from the console."

8

Happy Hour

"Tye's ass is probably driving from the school to the football field as we speak. Good for him. I do that shit too much."

"Girl you are supposed to be enjoying yourself. This is your weekend off. Here, drink this too, Samantha said as she handed Dee a fourth drink. You deserve the *Mom of the Year Award.* Two teenage boys, a preteen girl, and a sometimes baby daddy – drink girl, drink!"

Laughing out loud, Dee tipped her fruity yet powerful drink up, and took a few sips back-to-back. Glad to be back at her ol' stomping ground, Dee again scanned her surroundings - a wooden deck overlooking the beach, a big wraparound classy bar, some eye candy, and a lit DJ, just the remedy the doctor ordered.

"The kids are good. They are a lot of work, but they are good kids. God blessed me right with them."

I LOST MY MIND

"Til some crazy fast girls start chasing after your sons. And just wait til your sweet daughter starts her period. The shit will really hit the fan then. Trust me, I know."

"How are your kids doing anyway?"

"First year of college for my oldest, last year of high school for my middle, and six more months of probation for my youngest. My husband has been working out of town for the last three weeks. I was gonna go surprise his ass, but I can't leave my daughter unattended that long with this ankle monitor bullshit she got going on."

"Damn, that sucks! Now you gotta be the mom and the correction officer."

"Just when I was about to retire from being a homemaker and find a career to get plugged into – bam – she went crazy! She got like sixty hours of community service to do some damn where. I'll know soon enough because it will be my ass driving her back and forth."

Friday Night

9

Takeout

"Whatever you want. Go load up your box," Tye instructed his kids at the Chinese buffet.

First meal of the weekend - served!
Excellent job, Daddy!

"$96.62, sir."

Tye swiped his card, added a generous tip, which brought the total to $125.00, and smiled.

Shit! $125 for one meal. Sure enough, these kids will be ready to eat again, again, and again. . . Saturday and Sunday.

$125 Friday
$125 + $125 + $125 = $375 Saturday
$125 + $125 + $125 = $375 Sunday
$875 in takeout!
Woow, wooow, woooow! I need a better plan!

I LOST MY MIND

Everyone loaded into the car. Dominique grabbed Tye's phone out of the console, this time without asking.

So that's how it is? Do I say something or let it ride? She was in the middle of her show, so whatever.

As Tye drove, he glanced on and off in the rearview mirror at his two sons and reminisced - from car seats to teenagers. Tye noticed the boys *noticed* him looking at them. To make it less weird he asked, "How was football practice?"

"Good."

"Fine. We have an out-of-town tournament tomorrow. Did mom tell you? It is in Samsone."

"Samsone is almost an hour away. No, she didn't tell me. Are you sure you even mentioned it to her? Usually, she is nonstop texting me, play-by-play, when you all are with me dictating how we manage our time together. . . I haven't heard from her since she dropped you all off at school."

"That is because she got a new man," Dominique interjected, waiting for the *skip ad* box to pop up so she could get back to her show.

"What time do you all have to be there?"

"Games are at eight, nine, and ten. When we win at least two games, although we will probably win all three, we play again at three and five o'clock."

"So, we gotta leave the house by 7 a.m., be in the sun all day, and get home around 7 p.m.?"

"Coach wants us there by 7:15 a.m. to warm up. So, we gotta leave by six in the morning."

Dee pulled a fast one. She really tried me. An all-day-outdoor-hot-hot-hot-miserable-sweaty day.

Tye tried his best to sound enthusiastic, "Showers and bedtime after we eat this food! We have a big day tomorrow."

"What is this, Daddy?" Dominique asked curiously, finally looking up from the phone.

Oh shit! What popped up on the phone?

"Can we go? Can we go?" Dominique pleaded.

"I'm not sure what you are talking about, baby girl."

"This," Dominique exclaimed and held up the phone so Tye could see it:

10

Text-to-Text

> Dee, did you know that the boys have to be in Samsone in the morning for an all day football thing?

8:15 p.m.   **$$$ TYE $$$**

> ???

9:20 p.m. **$$$ TYE $$$**

> So you got jokes?

10:00 p.m. **$$$ TYE $$$**

> Oh yea, you off the grid.

11:02 p.m. $$$ TYE $$$

11:16 p.m.   Dee 🩷

Shit, my head is throbbing.
Too many. Too many.
I need some water!

"Bae, will you bring me some water?" Dee heard the TV on in the other room. That is what woke her up. "Bae?"

That loud ass TV done woke me up and now his ass acts like he can't hear.

I'm glad it ain't me going to the field tomorrow.

> Go to bed. You got a long day tomorrow. Drink plenty of water.

11:23 p.m.   Dee

I LOST MY MIND

Dee got out of bed to grab her purse. She needed to find her charger. Her cell phone battery was at three percent. She didn't like being at her new boyfriend's apartment. It was much too small and way too cluttered. It looked like a dorm room, even though it has probably been twenty years since he earned his master's degree.

Where is his ass at anyway? I haven't known him long enough to be alone at his apartment. Don't know much about his past. Anyone could pop up and pop off.

T.V. on. Several empty beer bottles on the counter.

I did my walk through in a few steps.
Nowhere to hide in this teeny-weeny ass place.

I'm not calling his phone. I'm too old to play tag.

Dee grabbed her stuff, a bottle of water, got in her car, and headed home.

11

Night-Night

Sitting on the edge of her bed, once again, Torie looked at the clock. This time it was after midnight and Torie was looking for her *nighttime* meds to be able to sleep.

It was a great day.
The kids enjoyed our time outside and so did I.
Thank God for the small moments of joy in this humongous mountain of darkness. Allie had a few hours to herself, which she so deserves, and I even made dinner. With all that good today, I thought I could half my nighttime med.
Not so.

I LOST MY MIND

Torie read the label on her prescription bottle and debated on doubling the dose so she could go to sleep and *not* dream about the fairytale life she once had.

> *Two tonight.*
> *I'll gradually go back to the prescribed amount next week. There is too much to face this week –*
> *the eleventh year anniversary of our first date.*
> *From first glance. . .*
> *To the last look before the casket closed. . .*

With a lump of grief in her throat, tears silently streamed down her face. Torie struggled to swallow her pills.

"God, help me," Torie whispered as she laid down with her face in the pillow on her husband's side of the bed.

Saturday Morning

12

Time Crunch

Eleven tabs opened at once, Conner clicked back and forth, and gathered research to add to the templates for his final project. Conner heard his father's alarm clock echo through the hallway.

What a way to spend my Friday night!
Already 4:30 a.m.

The same time his father has waken up six days a week, for as long as Conner could remember. Sundays, however, he sleeps in until 7 a.m.

He will be making coffee soon. When he walks down the hall, I'll ask him to please make enough for me as well. Good plan. I have to get a perfect score on this project to keep my 'A' average in this class. The teacher gave us til Saturday 9 a.m. to

I LOST MY MIND

turn it in. Boring topic. I still should have started working on it sooner.

"Son, please tell me you woke up early and have not been up all night."

"I woke up early and have not been up all night," Conner said with a half-smile. "Coffee?"

Both laughing, they walked to the end of the hall together, down the stairs, and into the kitchen. Dad gathered everything needed to prepare the coffee and Conner sliced a few bagels to put in the toaster oven. Mom set them up for success by putting a small red dot on the dial, right at the perfect time interval so the bagels came out slightly crispy but still soft in the middle.

As the bagels toasted and the coffee began to fill the pot, Conner watched his father open his planner and review his schedule for the day.

Consistent.
Predictable.
Productive.
Looking forward to every day.
Excited to get out of bed before the sun gets up.
Why? How?

"What is your secret to success, Dad?"
"What do you mean?"

"How are you not bored yet? You have the same routine every day. Start and end every day the exact same way. You could have retired a few years ago. I know you got plenty of money. You don't have to work. You could take it easy," Conner stopped talking to give his father a chance to respond.

"Yes, I start and end each day the same. Right here in this house with the people who are the most important to me. What I do throughout the day though, varies from day to day. The mission, however, is always the same. I thank God for His wisdom and the creative power He gives us. For the last eight years, God has enabled me to keep my business, His business, relevant, prosperous, and able to effectively meet the needs of His people."

"I didn't know you were so religious, Dad."

"I'm far from religious. Around the time you were going into high school, I experienced the absolute hardest time in my career. You know the company I worked for since before you were born?" Dad took a sip of his coffee and Conner shook his head, "They got to the point where they wanted me to start doing the unethical stuff the higher ups had been doing for years. I never liked what I *knew* was going on, but I put it to the back of my mind. I wanted to keep my paycheck and I figured if anyone ever asked, I would say 'I had no idea.' Since I wasn't directly involved, I justified my knowledge of it. Then they started putting pressure on me to partake in their crooked ways. I almost crumpled and compromised my integrity.

I LOST MY MIND

One evening, as I drove home from work, I scanned through the radio stations. All of the sudden, I heard a voice that captured my attention. I tuned in and listened to a pastor teach about the *Parable of the Talents*. Have you ever read it?

"No, where would I find it?"

"It is in the Bible. Matthew 25," Dad answered as he pulled his Bible out of his briefcase.

My dad carries a Bible in his briefcase. What? I did not know any of this.

"Read the highlighted verses," Dad said as he placed the open Bible next to Conner's bagel, covered with a light layer of plain cream cheese.

So, I'm an early morning, coffee drinking, bagel eating, Bible reader now?

were ready went in with him to the wedding; and the door was shut.
11 "Afterward the other virgins came also, saying, 'Lord, Lord, open to us!'
12 "But he answered and said, 'Assuredly, I say to you, ᴿI do not know you.' [Hab. 1:13]
13 "Watch therefore, for you know neither the day nor the hour* in which the Son of Man is coming.
14 "For *the kingdom of heaven is* like a man traveling to a far country, who called his own servants and delivered his goods to them. Matt. 21:33
15 "And to one he gave five talents, to another two, and to another one, ᴿto each according to his own ability; and immediately he went on a journey. [Rom. 12:6]
16 "Then he who had received the five talents went and traded with them, and made another five talents.
17 "And likewise he who *had* received two gained two more also.
18 "But he who had received one went and dug in the ground, and hid his lord's money.
19 "After a long time the lord of those servants came and settled accounts with them.
20 "So he who had received five talents came and brought five other talents, saying, 'Lord, you delivered to me five talents; look, I have gained five more talents besides them.'
21 "His lord said to him, 'Well *done,* good and faithful servant; you were faithful over a few things, I will make you ruler over many things. Enter into the joy of your lord.'
22 "He also who had received two talents came and said, 'Lord, you

---

*24:48 NU-Text omits *his coming.* 25:6 NU-Text omits *is coming.* 25:13 NU-Text omits the rest of this verse.

delivered to me two talents; look, I have gained two more talents besides them.'
23 "His lord said to him, 'Well *done,* good and faithful servant; you have been faithful over a few things, I will make you ruler over many things. Enter into the joy of your lord.'
24 "Then he who had received the one talent came and said, 'Lord, I knew you to be a hard man, reaping where you have not sown, and gathering where you have not scattered seed.
25 'And I was afraid, and went and hid your talent in the ground. Look, there you have what is yours.'
26 "But his lord answered and said to him, 'You ᴿwicked and lazy servant, you knew that I reap where I have not sown, and gather where I have not scattered seed. Matt. 18:32
27 'So you ought to have deposited my money with the bankers, and at my coming I would have received back my own with interest.
28 'Therefore take the talent from him, and give *it* to him who has ten talents.
29 ᴿ'For to everyone who has, more will be given, and he will have abundance; but from him who does not have, even what he has will be taken away. Matt. 13:12
30 'And cast the unprofitable servant into the outer darkness. There will be weeping and gnashing of teeth.'
31 ᴿ"When the Son of Man comes in His glory, and all the holy* angels with Him, then He will sit on the throne of His glory. [1 Thess. 4:16]
32 "All the nations will be gathered before Him, and He will separate them one from another, as a shepherd divides *his* sheep from the goats.

I LOST MY MIND

"The Holy Spirit continued to provoke me through that passage of Scripture for weeks, which became months. My whole life, higher ups told me how talented I was. I received promotion after promotion. As I got closer to the top, more and more corruption was revealed. A voice activated in my spirit that kept reminding me, *I had hidden my talent among the wicked and unprofitable*.

I was bringing a big fat zero return to God, who gave me the talents everyone else boasted about. During the early morning hours, I dedicated time to planning. Within seven months, I went from the fearful *what ifs* of potential failure to the hopeful *what if I never try*. I was adamant to *not* miss out on truly fulfilling my purpose. I just knew I had to try opening my own business.

All the amenities of my previous job, which I was terrified of walking away from, are now small in comparison to what God has given me.

To answer your question, God is the secret of my success. Fulfilling His purpose is never boring. It is essential and rewarding. What about you? Have you finalized your degree track yet?"

"Not yet, I told my advisor I will be back to meet with her this upcoming week."

13

Game Day

Dee woke up at home alone much earlier than planned. Not able to go back to sleep, she reached for her phone. It must not have been plugged in properly. At some point during the night, it powered down. She got out of bed and walked toward the kitchen.

Damn! So, this is how it would be with no kids and no man. I don't like the way this feels. Almost eerie. The house is still clean since ain't nobody been here, and I don't even have anyone to cook for.

The kids probably took Tye up through there this morning. They are a hard bunch to get moving and out of the house.

Dee plugged her phone into the charger, placed it on the kitchen counter, drank some water, thought about going to the gym, and then *thought* against it. Now leaned

I LOST MY MIND

on the counter, Dee powered her phone up and scanned through her missed text messages:

> So it's like that. . . ???

3:02 a.m.   **New Boo**

3:02 a.m.? Damn, you tried me. Ol' sorry ass. Thought I was gonna wait around all that time for him. He's gonna wish he never played that game.

> Dee, heading to Samsone. The boys wanted to pick up something from the house. NVM. We will figure it out.

5:45 a.m.   **$$$ TYE $$$**

Why text me if you are gonna NVM me?

> Beach today?

8:20 a.m.   **Samantha**

9:56 a.m.   **$$$ TYE $$$**

"Hello."

"Mom, are you coming to the field? I need you to bring me something."

"What? You know I wasn't planning on it. You all are with your father this weekend."

Dee's other son grabbed the phone to back up his brother, "Mom, we are still your kids. You don't ever miss a game."

"What is so important that you need me to drive way to Samsone to bring you?"

"*You,* mom! We wanted to pick *you* up and bring *you* with us."

"Don't ya all coach need you to run some drills or something?"

"Mom, please!"

"If you win this morning, maybe I'll come out this afternoon."

"We already won twice this morning, so please be here for our 3 p.m. game. Please."

"Bye boys! Love you all and tell Dominique I love her too."

END CALL

I LOST MY MIND

"Coach wants you all in the warmup area," Tye told the boys as he extended his hand to retrieve his phone. "What did your mom say?"

"She is coming."

To clarify, Tye asked, "Did she say she is coming?"

"No, but she will."

> Girl, I guess Stella ain't getting her groove back this weekend. I'm going to Samsone for the boys' afternoon game.

10:03 a.m.   **Dee** ♥

> Wear something to make Tye BREAK his damn neck! Drive safe!

10:05 a.m.   **Samantha**

> YA KNOW IT!

10:06 a.m.   **Dee** ♥

14

Knock Knock

"Mrs. Torie," Allie whispered as she knocked on the door of the master bedroom. Smiling across the room at Mrs. Torie's mother, Allie amplified her voice and knocked a little harder, "Mrs. Torie, your mom is here for a visit."

Allie knew Mrs. Torie would be horrified if her mother saw her, in what has become, her morning stupor.

"Just getting out of the shower, I will be right out," Torie yelled in the most upbeat voice she could mimic.

Not today! Why mother, why? Not today!

*I gotta jump out of bed, take a shower,
get dressed, and present myself sane
in the living room in five minutes. Minute six,
she will be pushing her way through the door.*

I LOST MY MIND

Gotta be out there by 10:52.
Ready.
Set.
Go.
Pills. Pills. Pills.

Adrenaline rushed thorough Torie's body. Her biggest fear was showing weakness in front of her mother. She didn't want her mom worrying about her.

"Good morning, mom! I'll be out in five minutes," Torie yelled as she quickly grabbed a sundress from her closet and beelined into the luxurious walk-in shower.

15

Concession Stand

Why is this line moving so slow?
Why is it so damn hot out here?

That is definitely Dee's favorite candy.
Should I get it and give it to her when she gets here?

Tye - are you a fool?
She is too prideful to take any kind gesture from you.

She surely takes my money though.

"Daddy, how many things can I get?"
"What did you have in mind?"
"Candy, nachos, and a drink."
"Sounds good to me. I will get the same. Should we get something to have ready for your mom when she gets here?" Tye asked Dominique in an indirect attempt to find out if she thought Dee was really coming.

I LOST MY MIND

"She doesn't like that fake nacho cheese, but she does like that candy right there. It is her favorite."

So, Dee is really coming. Exciting!

What if she is coming just to judge my parenting?

What if she goes off on me?

What if she has her hair up, curves on display, a pair of strappy sandals going up those just right calves, and glittering toes? She is fine, sexy, juicy, edible...

She better not come out here and try me. Better not bring no sorry ass man out here & act all brand new. I hope like hell she don't try me like that.

She does deserve better than me though. I could have done better by her. I should have done better. I would have done better if...

"Thirty-five dollars, sir," the volunteer at the concession stand landed Tye's wondering thoughts. "Would you like to make a donation to support the football league?"

$35.00 for $2.00 worth of food AND a donation? Whatever. Don't look like an asshole Tye.

Tye handed the elderly woman two twenty-dollar bills and directed her to put the change toward a donation.

With great enthusiasm, the commentator's voice boomed from the speakers. Tye's son just ran a touchdown into the endzone, and his other son threw the pass. Dominique shouted and jumped.

They definitely didn't get their athleticism from me. Am I really their daddy?

Yes, I am. Yes, I am!

If anything, I bought 'em with all that child support I pay.

16

I'm Ready

*You're dressed. You ate breakfast.
The kids look great. Allie did her thing, as usual.
Both girls look so adorable in their matching
sundresses and headbands. Mom doesn't
suspect anything except 'normal' grief.*

"Torie, let me take you and my granddaughters out of *this* house for a few days. We could go to a resort with a nice pool and an exploration area for the kids. Kickback, relax, laugh, and *not* look at all these memories around here."

No way! Can't do it!

First of all, you are too nosey and will eventually see my meds. Then you will tell me how much you disapprove of them and all the things I 'should' be doing to 'come back from this', instead of taking doctor prescribed medication.

Secondly, I need Allie to make me look good as a parent. I can't handle these two on my own.

I never could.
That is why we hired Allie.
We, my husband and I...

Am I still allowed to say, 'my husband' when he is dead?

Thankfully, a cup of juice dropped from the two-year old's hands and exploded on the floor, breaking up Torie's thoughts and giving her time to come up with a response to give her mother.

Allie moved into position to clean up the mess.

"I got it, Allie. Me and my mom are going to spend some time together today with the girls. Consider yourself free for the day, until around six o'clock, let's say?"

"Yes ma'am. I will take you up on that offer. I will be in my room for a little while then may head out. Have a great day," Allie said with a little bit of hesitation, nevertheless, glad to see Mrs. Torie making her day count.

As Allie headed to her room, the toddler ran over giggling and briefly hugged her leg. Allie looked back and saw Mrs. Torie cleaning up the spill and her mother holding the baby. All was well and Allie appreciated the unexpected time off.

Allie moved in as a part time nanny when Mrs. Torie was eight months pregnant with her youngest daughter. Mrs. Torie's husband hired her to help, anticipating the birth of the new baby, knowing the initial transition into stay-at-home mother was difficult for his wife with one child and now there would be two.

Mrs. Torie took an extended leave of absence from her career as a corporate executive. She is very educated, esteemed, accomplished, and beautiful.

Allie moved away from her family to attend college in the area. Their agreement was for all household expenses and Allie's cell phone bill to be paid for by the family; use of one of their cars; a private living area; and a generous monthly stipend to compensate Allie. In return, Allie committed to fulfill her role as the girls' nanny until they become school age.

It was the perfect opportunity for Allie. She is on a four-year degree track at the college and now has a home away from home. Originally, the plan was for Mrs. Torie to be solo Tuesday and Thursday mornings from 9 a.m. to noon, while Allie was on campus. Mondays and Wednesdays, Mrs. Torie was to relieve Allie and manage the kids alone from 3 p.m. until her husband arrived home. Those afternoons, Allie was free to complete her assignments and be online for her evening classes. Fridays and Saturdays, Allie worked no more than eight hours combined, as needed, so Mrs. Torie and her husband could be free for community obligations and various outings. Allie was always off on Sundays.

All that changed when Mrs. Torie's husband died. She increased Allie's stipend and recently hired a second nanny to be at the house from eight to four o'clock, Monday through Thursday. Simply put, now the nanny has a nanny.

A new semester just started, so Allie was able to adjust her schedule and maximize her time on campus. When at home, Allie continuously does almost everything for the children and maintains the household.

Saturday Afternoon

17

Mommy, Me, & Little Mes

The zoo? Really, Mom?
Does she realize we have two kids, both in car seats and diapers? At least I was able to talk my way out of the resort trip she suggested.

I have been to this zoo at least thirty times. My husband – my dead husband – was an integral part in establishing it. In return, they gave us an honorary lifetime family pass. Well, his lifetime ended, but we are still here.

Great.
All day, in my face, memories.
Condolences.
Every time someone recognizes me.
Condolences.

*How about you just let me try to enjoy
my children and myself for a second?*

*Nope.
Condolences.*

"Oh Mom, the zoo? Okay, now that the girls heard you mention it, there is no taking it back," Torie said forcing herself *not* to sound sarcastic. "I will get the 'go bag' packed. We should definitely take my SUV, since the car seats and double stroller are already in there."

"Don't forget the sunscreen. I'm gonna sneak out and . . .," Torie's mom made a silent, *I'm going to go smoke a cigarette* communication, that consisted of hand gestures and mute lip movements.

*Great.
So, I'm really taking three kids to the zoo.*

*Condolences.
Your husband was such a great man.
Condolences.
It was just horrible to hear, hang in there.*

*Yes, he was great!
YES, it is even MORE horrible to live without him.
Every single day.
Every single hour.
Every single minute.
Every single second.*

I LOST MY MIND

Torie threw whole boxes of toddler snacks into the bag, filled her daughter's *special* cup with cold water, and gathered all that is needed for the baby's bottles. Two sizes of diapers and wipes were already in the bag.

"Come on, sweetie. Let's get in the car. Grandma's waiting," Torie guided her toddler out the door, as she held the baby, and slung the bag over her shoulder.

Oh crap, the sunscreen!
I'll never live that down.
Forgetting the sunscreen.
Major mom foul.
God forbid they get a sunburn.
My mom will talk about me,
talk about me,
talk about me.

Let me get them secure in the car,
then I'll run back in.

18

Kick Off

I guess she is not coming.
Why I got all jittery – I don't know.

Hell. It has been hot as hell out here all day.
Thank God the sun will be dropping soon.

Just like Dee dropped my ass. I can't blame her though. Shit, I couldn't even stand myself.

I'm just thankful I can support my kids financially and rebuild a relationship with them.

She does get too much money though.
Nah – she don't get enough.
I could never repay her.
These kids are expensive and a whole lot of work.

I should be home right now – calm, cool, and collected. Instead, I'm hot, sweaty, and far from home.

I LOST MY MIND

"Mommy," Dominique yelled out and hopped down the bleachers, shaking Tye emotionally and physically.

How the hell are you gonna play this off, Tye?
She is gonna look good.

Shit! If I turn around and see her with some man, I'm gonna snap.

No, I'll go to the car.
No, I'll go to the bathroom and get my ass together.
. . . Come up with a plan.

First, I need to see what's up.
Turn around Tye and don't look like a creeper.

Tye turned his attention to Dominique, knowing he would catch a glimpse of Dee out of the corner of his eye and be better able to assess the situation.

"Domi. . .," Tye started to say.

Boy – ya, probably got drool going down the side of your mouth. Chill out.

No man insight. I hope one ain't parking the car.

Dee – girl, ya still got it. All of it.

Tye – ya look real stuck right now. Say something. Is she just here to make sure I'm taking care of the kids?

Is she here just to see the kids?

Maybe – is she here to see me?
No, she definitely didn't drive all this way to see me.

Stop staring. Say something.

"Good to see you, Dee," Tye said probably sounding way too enthusiastic. He then quickly turned his attention to the football field to avoid a prolonged awkward encounter. Not knowing much about football, Tye tried to look engaged.

Still fine. His ass is still fine. Definitely.
Still fit. His ass is still fit. Definitely.
Still financially sound. That money comes on time.
Does he have anything else to say?
It has been a long-long while. Too long.
I guess long enough.
I guess I will never know all the 'whys' I have wondered...

Dee and Dominique climbed up a few rows on the bleachers and sat in front of Tye.

Give her the candy.
No, that is too corny.
Just chill.

I LOST MY MIND

"Mom, Daddy got you this candy," Dominique said as she handed her mom the open candy bag.

"So you tried it already?" Dee gave a sly smile and got a few pieces out for herself. "How are your brothers doing? Obviously, the team has been winning."

"Doing their thing as usual. What have you been doing, Mom?"

Minding my grown business.
Or more like trying to 'not' be grown.

"Not much. Saw some friends last night and now here I am," Dee put her arm around Dominique then quickly realized it was too hot to be hugged up.

"We are going to church tomorrow with dad."

Holy shit! What did that girl just say? I hope he ain't about to die or something. He looks healthy.

Dee turned her head to double check Tye's appearance. She wanted to make sure she didn't miss any signs of illness.

"Yes, it's true. And no, I ain't dying, Dee," Tye said with a serious face and a smile in his eyes. "My coworker has been on me to go and Dominique saw the flyer. There is a field day BBQ thing after church. The kids thought it looked cool, so we will check it out."

"Good to hear," Dee responded a little unsure of who this coworker was who apparently influenced her family.

It better not be no female trying to pounce on the greatness growing here. No predatory ass cougar is gonna eat of this feast.

Saturday Night

19

Saturday Night Decisions

Dad was on the back patio with mom winding down from their day. They are such a great team. Very rare to see. Being an adult now, Conner appreciates his parents' solid marriage even more than when he was a child.

So committed.
Committed to marriage.
Committed to family.
Committed to home.
Committed to career.
Now, I'm finding out, committed to God.
So, why am I so indecisive?

Talent – come out wherever you are!
I just have to be sure.
I definitely don't want to bury my talent in an unprofitable place.

Conner motioned to his parents, through the oversized patio door, he was heading out. Not to hang out with friends, but to drive around the city and try to see himself *somewhere*. Another thing his father told him during their conversation this morning was, "When a man doesn't know where he is going, everywhere looks the same."

Sunday Morning

20

Pancakes!

Dominique entered Tye's room as he slept and approached the side of his bed.

"Daddy," she whispered then playfully raised her voice, "pancakes, pancakes, PANCAKES!"

Tye woke up laughing. "My baby girl! You just took me back some years. You used to do the same thing when you were like three years old. Are your brothers up yet?"

"They are still snoring and farting."

Tye laughed again. "You are quite amusing this morning my love! Pancakes it is. I'm gonna jump in the shower and I will be out in fifteen minutes."

"Put your church clothes on, Daddy. So, we can go to that thing," Dominique directed Tye as she energetically exited the room.

That 'thing' that I hoped you forgot about. Dang. She always knows how to get me. When she was three, it was Dee getting up to make the pancakes. All I did was spray the whipped cream. Now, I gotta figure this out.

I probably don't even have everything I need to make pancakes. Shit. I should have made an eating plan for these kids.

Now I understand why Gramps always told my momma we 'eat him out of house and home'.

"Dominique," Tye yelled from the toilet. "Wake your brothers up, please. We are going out to breakfast before church."

Yeah, Tye – leave the pancake making to the professionals.

Ha, ha – ya' ass is gonna be at church all day and now Steven is gonna expect you there every Sunday. Probably gonna wanna have Bible study in the conference room every day at work.

I should have just gotten Dominique her own phone. Then she wouldn't have had my phone in her hand when Steven texted me that stupid flyer.

After quickly progressing through his morning routine, Tye exited his room ready for the day. He secretly *hoped* Dominique couldn't get the boys up and went back

I LOST MY MIND

to sleep herself. No such luck. All three of them were dressed, shoes on, and sitting on the couch waiting.

How the hell did Dee raise these kids so good?
Prompt.
Prepared.
Good hygiene.
Well mannered.
All while I've been about some bullshit for the last seven years. I missed so much. Too much.

"Dad, why are you looking at us like *that*?" Tye's son asked with a weird look on his face.

"I just can't believe how much you all have grown up. And grown up right! Thank God for your mother. Let's go."

21

Rise & Fall

Yesterday was good. Very good. Surprisingly.
Only like five condolences.
Some sincere. Some out of obligation.
Whatever. Glad it is over.
Mom didn't suspect anything.
I'm starting to realize she is too
busy hiding her own issues.
The kids did great. I did great. I'm glad we went.

Today is a new day & it feels like a total downer.
Sundays used to be our family day.
No work. No interruptions.
My husband actually silenced all his

I LOST MY MIND

electronics from sunup to sundown.
He would only check his email and alerts before
bed to finalize Monday's agenda.
So disciplined.
So successful.
So caring.
The love of my life.

Torie entered her bed last night at eight o'clock p.m. and is still exhausted. She rolled over in bed to keep her husband's picture out of view. Desiring to be at peace in her sleep, Torie had just taken another one of her *nighttime* pills, even though it was morning. She needed more rest.

22

Church

Breakfast was good.
Food = good.
Kids' conversation = good!
It was never my intention to be a sorry ass father.

Dang, Steven spotted us quick. Shit, does he have a GPS tracker on me?

Same old flip flops and a more casual button up. Is that his wife? How the hell did he pull her? Look at his kids . . . three like me. Much younger though.

Steven approached as if he was cued, "Tye, so glad you made it. Welcome."

Tye shook Steven's extended hand. Steven then extended his hand to each of Tye's children. "This is my wife, Cleopatra, and my three minis."

I LOST MY MIND

Tye quickly said hello to each of them and watched his sons greet Steven and his family with such etiquette. Dominique, with her sweet demeanor, was more brief like Tye, and gave a courteous smile.

The usher gave Tye a first-time visitor card and walked them through the large double doors and down the aisle to be seated. Steven and his family continued to welcome people as they arrived in the lobby.

Please don't go any further down the aisle. Here is fine. We don't need to be too close to the front. Come on . . . the back is good.

Here, the middle – definitely the perfect spot. No need to go any further.

Stop. Stop. Here we go. Please, stop!

"Can we sit right here on the end, please?" Tye asked, trying not to offend the usher or sound like a heathen.

"Of course, we can walk your daughter to children's church and your sons to Teens-4-Christ."

Tye looked at his children to *read* their faces. They didn't show any nonverbal resistance. "Do you want to go or sit with me?" Tye asked hoping at least one out of the three of them would sit with him.

"Sure, we would love to participate. Thank you," Tye's son responded as he motioned to his brother and sister to follow the usher.

So, my ass is sitting here alone.
Get your mind right, Tye. You are in church.
I mean: So, I'm sitting alone.

Tye knew Steven and his wife were now seated and much closer to the front. He couldn't make eye contact with Steven, otherwise he would try to get Tye to sit up there with them. Tye silenced his phone and acted like he was a regular church attender.

It is pretty cool in here now, but is it gonna get hot?
Am I supposed to ask the usher for a 'church fan'?

23

Virtual

I'll be damned if my family is gonna be initiated into some cult. I need to know what the hell is going on.

Dee got just enough information about this church *thing* to find the online stream of the service.

Yesterday was good. The boys' team placed first in the tournament. The kids tried to rally Dee to go out for dinner and ice cream with them. She gave the excuse of being tired and not wanting to be on the road too late, in order to give Tye his space and his time with the kids.

Shit, his ass can't make up for these missed yearsSS.

At least he's tryna do something. Better not be too brand new though. Damn sure better not be tryna do better for some new coworker chick.

Dee was comfortably propped up in her bed, a cup of coffee on her nightstand, a deep conditioning treatment in her hair, and the virtual service cast from her phone to her fifty-eight-inch flatscreen.

The countdown clock had a handful of seconds left. The graphics were modern and appealing. A quick intro video concluded, and live music exploded through the speakers. The cinematic effects were motion picture like.

Now, this is a little too much. How much of the Lord's money do they spend on all this?

Tye better not be all leaning in on his holy ol' church inviting coworker - lurker chick in front of my kids.

Ten minutes of singing passed. Ain't heard none of those songs before. Nothing alarming. Overall, nice.

This must be the pastor's hype man on now. I would cuss, but not while watching church. This joker has the people hollering.

Here, he goes – this must be the pastor. Dressed kinda casual. Not sweating or breathing hard. Calm. Confident. Cool. Whatcha got to say?

Dee listened intently to the teaching. Every time the pastor read a Scripture it showed up on the screen. Eager to ensure her kids weren't at a crazy church, Dee followed

I LOST MY MIND

along and found herself surprisingly engaged in the teaching.

The sermon series was titled: *The Courage to NOT Do.* They even had a slide for guided notes. Everything was relatable and deliberately focused Dee's thoughts on certain situations in her life.

Increasing Like Jesus
The Courage to NOT Do...

- Do what is comfortable, familiar, and routine
- Remain in the *known* place of fear & doubt because the future is intimidating (escape route is intimacy with God)
- Settle in the convenient place when God is leading you into the covenant place

OPPORTUNITY

OP - a set of planned actions for a particular purpose

PORT - an opening (an entry point)

UNITY - the quality or state of not being multiple: **ONENESS**

The courage to NOT do.
Plenty.
There are plenty of things I need the courage to NOT do: Things that make me miserable. Things that initially sound good but are neither sound nor good. Preach, preacher! I can make a list of at least ten things right now. Maybe twenty-five.

"As long as you conform to an unprofitable place, there will be weeping and gnashing of teeth. Not only in the afterlife, but in this life. On the contrary, when you use your talents to glorify the Father, you *gain* a return and enter into the joy of the Lord. Turn with me to Mathew chapter twenty-five. Let's begin reading, starting at verse fourteen," the pastor led the congregation as they read to verse thirty together. He stopped a few times to emphasize his sermon points.

"I release to you today, by the power of the Holy Ghost, the courage to *not* do. The courage to escape fear and leave the convenient place in order to move into the covenant place. The text clearly says the person was fearful. Fear caused them to bury their talent in an unprofitable place. Don't be wicked and lazy. Do the necessary work to transform the wicked twisted mind. My God has not given us a spirit of fear, but of power and of love and of a sound mind. . ."

> Sis, let's get lit! Today is the last day of your va-cay! Perfect weather, too!

12:05 p.m.   Samantha

Look how the devil just popped up on my TV screen in the middle of the good part.

Dee swiped the message closed to get it off the screen but missed the Scripture reference for the last point.

I LOST MY MIND

I can rewind it back later. I definitely need to hear all of this again and again.

"The things you *think* you can't afford; others are *gaining* by trading their talents with one another. Most celebrities don't pay for the bling they wear on TV, although they could afford it. They don't pay the high price you or me would pay, because they trade their platform, built by their talent, to showcase the jewelry.

Check this out, if one person has mastered the craft of landscaping and another person has mastered the art of barbering, you have two households with well-manicured yards and on-point haircuts. Why? Because they hooked one another up by *trading* their talents.

When you are working for the middleman, your time is exchanged for limited money – what they *feel* like giving you, after they have gotten theirs.

The Holy Spirit is challenging us to put a demand on our God-given talent to gain wealth – to gain abundance. Your talent will produce for the sake of the covenant. I have three final Scriptures to share quickly this morning. Let's read Deuteronomy 8:18, Proverbs 10:22, Proverbs 18:16 together:

> Deuteronomy 8:18 "And you shall remember the LORD your God, for *it is* He who gives you power to get wealth, that He may establish His covenant which He swore to your fathers, as *it is* this day.

Proverbs 10:22 The blessing of the Lord makes *one* rich, and He adds no sorrow with it.

Proverbs 18:16 A man's gift makes room for him, and brings him before great men."

The pastor closed the message with a prayer and asked if there was anyone who wanted to give their life to Jesus Christ or recommit their talents to Him. The virtual screen saver came on for privacy. Dee could no longer see the service, but she could still hear the audio.

"Welcome, yes keep coming. The altar is open. The altar is a place of altering. Reposition yourself. God is realigning and reassigning many things. If you are online right now, and the spirit of God is talking to you, please type your name in the comments."

The comments were flooding in. Names were popping up and quickly being pushed up the screen, as more names took their positions. Dee typed her name.

24

Coincidence or Purposeful

After Conner typed his name in the comments, he was immediately relieved. He tangibly felt the pressure that tried to crush him anytime he had to make a decision about his future, lift off his shoulders. He committed to God's plan for his life. Conner would no longer consider every road he passed as a possible route. God is officially his GPS. Conner will trust Him to point out and navigate *the* significant roads – those that are right for him. Conner vowed to put an end to the distractions, confusion, and exhaustion of all the potential *good* options, and only focus on what is *right* for him. He will reserve his effort and energy to live his life *of* purpose, *on* purpose.

Conner reflected on how he spent his time last night. He pulled out of the driveway, after saying goodbye to his parents, and drove. He wasn't sure of his destination.

Conner was stopped at the stop sign, to exit his gated residential neighborhood, for about thirty seconds. Before he released his foot from the brake, Conner said out loud,

"God, you helped my father, please give me a glimpse of my future."

Always intrigued by the upbeat pace of the downtown area, Conner headed that way. He began to imagine a *day in the life* of finally grown-up Conner.

He intentionally looked at every building and structure he passed. There was a lot of unique and modern landscaping, as well as, ongoing construction projects.

Definitely don't see myself working outside at all. I tremendously appreciate everyone who does. They have the strength, stamina, and drive to do that, but it is not for me.

Conner noticed more counseling centers and children's programs than ever before. He read as many signs as he could and gave each business name, logo, motto, and graphic, a unique Conner rating in his head.

- ✓ *Is the signage noticeable and engaging?*
- ✓ *Does it quickly let people know what takes place there?*
- ✓ *Is it up to date or weathered?*
- ✓ *Is it readable from a distance and at night?*

Retail stores, a law firm, doctors' offices, cafes, diners, restaurants, a bakery, a fitness center, a tattoo parlor, several bars, a cigar shop – all these places and more are in a one-mile radius. What makes one place stand out from another?

I LOST MY MIND

Conner parked and walked around, although going nowhere specific. He purposefully paid attention to what businesses were opened or closed and busy or slow.

The corporate executive offices in the multi-story buildings were not opened on the weekends. He tried to see what types of companies were located there but had a hard time identifying the kind of business that transpired in each suite from day to day.

Bulbs were out in the free standing, three feet by three feet, *lit* directory map of the business complex. There were also a few cracks in it and most of the information did not match the few signs some doors did have. Obviously, it was outdated and made it hard for anyone to differentiate one business from another. Conner could only infer what services were offered in a couple of the catalysis of someone's dream from the courtyard. Conner hoped to locate *thee* office he wanted to walk into every day, however he was disappointed.

Conner returned to his car and removed a flyer from his windshield. As he glanced over it, he purposely decided to tune into the virtual broadcast of the church service he was just *anonymously* invited to.

The next morning, Conner was shocked as he listened to the pastor's teaching, using the same Scriptures his own father shared with him the morning before.

Conner was beyond any doubt, now fully convinced, God already had every detail of his life measured, marked, and mapped.

Conner opened another window on his laptop, went to his college's homepage, clicked on the degree programs tab, and browsed.

No.
No.
No.
No.
No.
What is that?
No.
Business Administration.
Marketing – a bachelor's degree?
Huuummmm.
Wow.
Read more, there has to be something bad about it.

I like it, sounds interesting.

How many of the many, many, many classes I have taken count toward this?

Quite a bit, it looks like.

Click on the video. Find out what you don't like about it.

Still looks good.

I LOST MY MIND

How much does it pay?
$65k and up. Reasonable starting pay. Growing industry.
I could work for a big or small company.
Or freelance.
Or establish my own business.
Definitely,
              definitely,
                            definitely!
I will talk to Ms. Matthews about this first thing tomorrow morning!

==Sunday Night==

25

Home Sweet Home

How is this car so full, yet so silent? I know I got all the kids. I triple checked. Dominique sang that song today! Hopefully my sunglasses fortified my tearing eyes. The boys impressed everyone with their athleticism, but more importantly with their sportsmanship and willingness to help coach the little kids.

How do I just jump back into their life? Would Dee let me be more a part of their life after I was the one who broke their life apart?

Never. Never has she kept them from me. Talked trash, yea – a whole lot. Never kept them from me though.

That was me. Do the kids even know where I have been? Somehow, my reputation with them has remained untainted. Dee must not have told them

I LOST MY MIND

everything. Obviously, I can't ask them. Then they would know.

How do I thank Dee for all she has done for me and the kids without her thinking I'm just trying to creep back in?

I must keep my commitment to the group of men I talked to today at church. Tuesday nights. Twice a month – Emphasize the Dash Men's Fellowship. Make the dash between my date of birth and date of death count.

> Ten minutes away.
> Kids are knocked out.

7:50 p.m.   **$$$ TYE $$$**

> I'll meet you at the house in 20 minutes. In route.

7:53 p.m.   **Dee**

Well, where you at? None of my business.

> Okay.

7:54 p.m. **$$$ TYE $$$**

26

Around the Corner

Dee looked in the mirror and ensured she looked good. She was not going for the *I did extra special for you look*. Her goal was the *I always look good - a natural beauty lifestyle look*.

Next, she turned the lights off, grabbed her purse and keys, then quickly got into her car and backed out of the garage. Briefly, Dee debated which way she should go because she didn't want Tye to see her pulling out of her neighborhood.

Childish, yes!

But I don't want him thinkin' I've just been sitting around the house waiting on him to drop the kids off all day. I gotta life too. He ain't the only one.

And he better not pull up with his church invitin' coworker cougar. She better never – never have even been in the car with my kids.

I LOST MY MIND

Dee was very familiar with the city she lived in for her entire life. She maneuvered through a twenty-minute course and pulled back up in her driveway. As anticipated, Tye was already in the driveway, pulled over just enough for her to pull her car into the garage.

Thank God it is just him and the kids – no undesirable guest.

Girl, you know him. He was all kinda fluttered yesterday. Get out of the car just right. Yup!

Dee featured her bare leg out of the car first and dropped her hips a little bit as she got out slowly. While she was doing it to be seen, she acted like she wasn't doing it on purpose.

Dee, cute and intentionally, made the one hundred eighty degrees turn, necessary to face Tye's car.

I know the kids see me. Time to go. Don't make me come over there. Just pop the trunk Tye and kick them out of the car. Like an ol' VHS on stop, everything was shaky, yet still.

Dee waved her hand for the kids to get out of the car. Tye rolled down the window, "Hang on Dee, they are coming. I'm giving them their lunch money for the week."

Dee couldn't help but laugh and walked over to the passenger side of the car.

Within a few minutes, Dee and the kids were back in the house. The kids told Dee all about their afternoon at church. They didn't mention the coworker and Dee knew she shouldn't put *that* pressure on the kids by asking.

27

Thank You

> Thank you, Dee.
> You have done a whole lot that you didn't have to do.

11:05 p.m.   **$$$ TYE $$$**

> And you have done a whole lot because I didn't do what I was supposed to do.
> Thank you!

11:06 p.m.   **$$$ TYE $$$**

It's hard to compile a stank response when I heard that good word today on virtual church. And I truly see he is doing his best to make up for lost time.

Seven years ago, criminal charges were being drawn up against Tye for some type of financial mishap. As his defense attorney recommended, they quickly divorced in an attempt to protect assets and distance Dee and the kids from the looming consequences of any such case.

It was the hardest thing Dee ever experienced in her life up until that point. The years that followed, however destroyed Dee internally. No one would know it by looking at her exterior.

The house was in her name and paid off several years before the criminal accusations were made. Dee was twenty-two when they were married, and Tye was twenty-five. Tye spent a lot of time with his grandparents when he was young, so he was very familiar with stuffing envelopes full of cash and stashing them around the house *for a rainy day.* That is the savings plan he used to buy Dee's first ever brand-new car on their third wedding anniversary. Years later, she eventually traded it in and now makes car payments like others who don't use an ol' fashion disciplined savings plan.

Tye was sentenced to three years in prison, then spent two years completing a work release program. Both were located four and a half hours from home. Because of the circumstances, they had to be very cautious and limit their communications. They only focused on the kids to legitimize their divorce and kept their distance as the high dollar attorney advised.

I LOST MY MIND

If it was up to Dee, none of that would have happened. She knew Tye was innocent, but the attorney said he would be found guilty by association, if he went to trial. Dee didn't want to get the divorce. She didn't want Tye to sign the plea deal. But it was out of her control.

At a young age, Dee married a good man, started a family right away, twin boys and a little girl four years later. She then ended up a single mother of three with an incarcerated ex-husband.

As directed by the attorney, Dee filed for child support. The dollar amount was set as high as possible, in order for a majority of Tye's money to legally become Dee's, just in case a future civil lawsuit was ever filed by the plaintiff in the criminal case. Five years passed. Tye moved back into the area and spent the last two years reestablishing himself.

The pain, life lessons, mistakes, destructive choices to produce brief counterfeit moments of happiness must be a thing of the past. What is my talent?

Raising phenomenal kids – ready for life, who will not bow, bend, or break when the going gets tough.

Before I move to take my rightful position as Tye's wife, I must heal from this self-inflicted heartache and genuinely forgive.

I'm coming for ya! Restoration is our portion. My role in my family is my profitable place. The words of a high dollar attorney will no longer limit me and my family. Besides, over the course of time, I've been paid way better than that attorney.

> You're welcome. Invite me out to dinner this week. Me and you.

11:25 p.m. Dee

28

Monday Morning

Allie opened the door for Dee with the baby in her arms. It was only Dee's second week being the 'nanny's nanny' as Allie called it. Dee sensed Allie was withholding a lot of information but didn't want to get *all up in* the household business in a pushy way.

Allie briefed Dee and showed her some of the food options she premade for the kids. She also let Dee know that Mrs. Torie did not come out of her room at all yesterday and she is not sure if Mrs. Torie even ate the meal she left on her nightstand yesterday afternoon.

Allie had quietly gone in and delivered a tray when Mrs. Torie was sleeping. Otherwise, Mrs. Torie would have rejected any form of help for herself.

Allie left within ten minutes of Dee getting there. Dee carried the baby to the swivel saucer play station and put her in it. Glad to have her freedom, the baby joyfully reached from one item to the next.

The toddler was sleeping on the extended chaise attached to the couch. Dee comfortably sat down and propped her legs up to make a barrier between the child and the floor to ensure there would be no falls on her shift.

Dee heard muffled whimpering. She could clearly see it was not the children. The sound came from the other side of Mrs. Torie's closed door.

The kids are light work.

My assignment is behind that door.

Did God just tell me that?

29

Lunch is Served

Giggles, quick light footsteps. Just a little fussing on and off. Sounds like the new nanny is doing good. The baby got used to her quick.

Allie snuck this food in here yesterday and it has been sitting there all night. Ewww. I don't need bugs in here.

I gotta get myself together and go to the kitchen. This is embarrassing. What is this lady gonna think?

Torie went through her pathetic morning routine. She begged herself to get up. Ingested her *new* life in pill form.

Showered and put on some activewear, in attempt to motivate herself to do something. Looked in the mirror, applied some brow pomade and lip gloss, while she hosted her own internal pep rally.

This is the plan Torie:
1. *Get this old food out of here.*
2. *Make small talk with the new nanny so she doesn't think you are a nutcase.*
3. *Bring the kids out back to give the nanny a break. She deserves it!*

Torie exited her bedroom with the tray. She hoped the nanny would think it was today's breakfast and not yesterday's one meal delivered to her solitary confinement cell. The kids saw Torie and automatically had a positive response. Torie smiled and felt normal for a few seconds. She quickly disposed of the food on the tray and directed her attention to her children. Now time for number two on her list, *make small talk with the new nanny.*

"Thank you for dedicating your time to help with the kids. I appreciate it more than you know." Torie felt surprisingly comfortable with Dee and effortlessly began to say more than she initially intended, "I used to have my life more together."

"Life happens. I've been a single mother of three for the last seven years. I never expected my marriage to end."

"My husband died."

"That sucks."

I LOST MY MIND

"Yes, it does. I appreciate your authenticity. Most people uncomfortably fumble for words, overtalk, insincerely wish their condolences, and share ten minutes of advice on a subject they have never dealt with. My husband dying in the prime of his life, leaving me with two small kids, is not the same as their dead dog or their dead grandma."

"Agreed, for sure. I have a *not* so healthy meal in route. Definitely enough for both of us. Do you want to eat together on the patio and the kids can play outside?" Dee offered.

"Are you sure you don't want to take a break? I can relieve you for an hour."

"No ma'am. I had a long enough break this weekend and I did not like it," Dee smirked to herself as she walked to the front door to retrieve the food that just arrived.

30

Dinner Plans

What a Monday!

Steven asked me if I enjoyed the service.
Then he asked me what I thought of the church.
Then he asked me what I thought of the message.
Then he asked me if I thought I would bring the family back.

Yes.
Good.
Good.
If only he knew how much I desired to have my family together.

I need to ask Steven some questions, but I don't know if he will give me real advice or a sermon point. I need an unbiased married man's opinion.

If I start a conversation with him, he might never shut up. It's toward the end of the day. He always *leaves here promptly at 4:00 p.m. I'm gonna go talk to him at 3:45. That way, he will keep it short and to the point - I hope.*

Tye finished running required reports and sent out a few emails to confirm the rest of the week's appointments. He looked at the clock and it was 3:41 p.m. Right on schedule to casually talk to Steven. Tye shutdown his laptop, slide it into the carrying case, then grabbed his cell phone and keys.

As he walked a few doors down to Steven's office, Tye was still unsure of exactly what he was going to say. Usually, he did his best to avoid Steven. Tye listened carefully as he approached Steven's office to make sure he wasn't in the middle of a virtual meeting or on the telephone.

About twenty people work in their office and somehow Steven always knows when Tye is approaching. Steven called Tye's name. For once, Tye was glad Steven initiated a conversation. They briefly discussed a mutual project.

"What is on your mind, Tye?" Steven asked sensing Tye had more on his mind and heart than work.

"I really don't have anyone to talk to about this. I need some man-to-man advice. Like your real-life opinion. Not a Bible verse."

"I'm a real-life man. I'll do my best. What's up?"

"You met my kids yesterday. Their mother is the love of my life. We got married when I was twenty-five years old. The minute I saw her, I knew she was the one. I worked with her brother, and she stopped by our job from time to time. Friendly greetings turned into meaningful conversations. Her brother thought good enough of me to eventually invite me to a holiday family BBQ. She was there. We talked. We laughed. We bonded. Her family recognized we had an authentic connection. Six months later we started planning our wedding. Everything I wanted to be as a husband, everything I wanted to do for my wife, became our reality little by little, year by year. We increased to a happy loving family of five.

Because of my ignorance, I turned a blind eye to financial woes transpiring among my corporate partners. I was innocent in action, but guilty by association because I didn't act. I couldn't bear the worst-case scenario option if the case went to trial, so I signed a plea. Five years away from my family.

My attorney advised an immediate divorce as soon as he became aware charges were going to be filed against me. He said that was his *off the record* man to man recommendation and he would do the same thing if it was him, to protect his wife, kids, and assets.

I've been back in the area, as you know, for the last two years. The work release program I was in, helped me secure this job.

I LOST MY MIND

The attorney scared me so bad about possible civil charges being brought against me in the future. He said that would financially bankrupt my family. Because of my fear, my family has been emotionally bankrupt, actually robbed. We all have suffered. I have had to suppress every desire embedded in me to be the husband and father I once was. According to the attorney, it is in our best interest that I just pay child support and see the kids on a rigid schedule, so the divorce looks legit. I broke my vows to my wife."

Tye's eyes erupted with tears. One after the other, tear drops slid from his eyes, and down both of his cheeks simultaneously, until he wiped them on the back of his hand. "She didn't want the divorce. I made her a single mother of three. I never wanted her to bear *that* reproach or have a reputation of not being one hundred percent loved, cared for, and totally supported by the man whose children she bore. We drifted so far apart, and it is my fault. I left her to navigate everything on her own. I want her back, but she deserves so much better than me. I caused so much turbulence in her life."

"Real life man to man," Steven interrupted, "my wife, the one you met yesterday. She took me back. We had a wedding date. Everything was all set and paid for. A week before the wedding, I freaked out. I had no idea what a husband even did. I was surrounded by women growing up. Everything I heard about men was a complaint. The few positive men in my community, I only saw at school or at sporting events. I did not see their interactions as husbands or fathers. Long story short, the wedding was cancelled. She didn't speak to me for over a year.

I ended up at the same church you were at yesterday. I made a quality decision to surround myself with men of integrity. They helped build me up. Then they told me to go find my wife and put in the hard work I was too scared to do before. Tye, I'm telling you the same thing. Never let fear control your relationship. Perfect love casts out all fear. It's 4:00. I gotta get home to my bride and you have plans to make."

Tye and Steven walked out of the building together. Steven texted his wife to let her know he was in route and planned to pick up dinner. Tye texted Dee.

> Any time.
> Any place.
> I ONLY want to be where you are.

4:12 p.m.   **$$$ TYE $$$**

About the Author

The two Scriptures that transformed my mind:

The thief does not come except to steal, and to kill, and to destroy. I have come that they may have life, and that they may have it more abundantly.

-John 10:10

What fruit did you have then in the things of which you are now ashamed? For the end of those things is death.

-Romans 6:21

Diana Robinson is a Bible teacher anointed to boldly declare destiny despite developmental delays. Her foundational beliefs include, "The Word of God is a *must* and diligently doing the Word will exempt you from every disqualification."

Under the leadership of Pastor Errol and Kim Beckford, Diana has grown into the precepts for her life: Associate Pastor (Celebration Tabernacle Church); wife (Michael Robinson); mother (Dia & Joy); grandmother (Ace & Delilah); author (The Robe of Many Colors, Exploring the Fruits of the Spirit with Joy, The Believer's Authority: How to Overcome Bible Study Series, Gaining Strength for Your Journey, I Write What is Right! 26 A-Z Daily Affirmations for Children, I Write What is Right! Cursive Edition Devotional Journal for Tweens & Teens); business owner (Transformed Publishing); and radio show co-host (Make Your Day Count).

I Lost My Mind is a series of fiction, yet factual books to help overcome the maze of the mind. *Tied, Destroyed, Tormented, & Confused* is the first book in the series. Please be on the lookout for book two coming September 2022, *Rebellious, Alone, Skeptical, & Dissatisfied*.

Please visit **www.transformedpublishing.com**

Exploring the Fruits of the Spirit with Joy
Diana Robinson, July 2020

Relevant and engaging for children of all ages. Use this book to teach, empower, and talk to your children about making Jesus' PEACE a reality by choosing to be full of joy and love, even when things do not go their way.

My Story: How God Delivered, Healed, & Set Me Free
Tawnya J. Jackson, October 2020

♦ Are you a single parent?
♦ Are you in a questionable relationship?
♦ Are you tired of being sick & tired?
♦ Are you experiencing depression, an unplanned pregnancy, or have a life changing decision to make?
♦ Is devastation or grief encroaching on your peace, purpose, or quality of life?
♦ Are things taking place in your life that you do not understand?

This book is for you. In, **My Story**, Tawnya Jackson honestly shares her heart and transition from despair and hopelessness to deliverance, healing, and freedom. **My Story** is full of strength, inspiration, and wisdom. It is a must read!

A Glimpse Into My Heart
Babette Bailey, November 2020

A Glimpse Into My Heart is a collection of poems sparked by many different people, events, hopes, dreams, issues, and a lot of other things that have touched & impacted Babette's heart in different ways.

Just like our lives, like a good song, or like a fresh new idea that could go on and on in our minds, these glimpses are meant to open the heart, gently lift the heart, and bring a spark to the heart that will go on and on.

The Believer's Authority
Diana Robinson, November 2020

- You are God's Masterpiece.
- You are the Apple of His Eye.
- You are an Expression of the Love of Jesus Christ.
- You were sent by the Lord to the earth for a Divine Purpose.
- You are here to manifest the vision that He wrote about you in the books of heaven before you were even formed in your mother's womb.
- You have been given authority, power, and access to live a victorious life.

Q: Do you believe this, but need help with unbelief?
A: This Study Guide, Workbook, & Journal is for you!

This Study Guide, Workbook, & Journal is broken down into six sessions. It is recommended that you spend an entire week of devotional time studying, meditating, praying, and journaling on each topic. Additional journaling pages are located in the back of this book.

From Servants to Sons
Diana Hicks, December 2020

- Sonship Brings Glory
- Sonship Brings Security
- Sonship Brings Faith
- Sonship Brings Authority
- Sonship Brings the Likeness of Jesus Christ

From Servants to Sons shares important truths to activate the authority and inheritance we already have in Jesus Christ.

Through Sonship, we are heirs in the family of God. This book will help you discover your covenant rights as Sons of God. This is not the time to give up but to push and to establish a real relationship with God. It is time to seek the Lord. To partake of this next season, we must become Sons of God. As a Son, you are to fulfill the Father's purpose.

Mamudah The Great One!
T. Benton-Parker, February 2021

Many children aspire to play professional sports. Mamudah is proof that with hard work and a positive attitude, childhood goals can be achieved.

This story demonstrates perseverance in action. Studying and doing your chores with excellence produces great results over time. Treating others with fairness and kindness brings great reward. Practicing your God-given talents and relentlessly pursuing your goals helps bring them to reality.

Preparing for the Real World Workbook
Lavica Chandler, February 2021

A workbook designed to teach children how to create a lifetime plan toward learning specific methods about spending and saving, budgeting, separating their wants and needs, and how to overcome overspending.

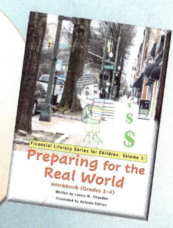

In the Shadows of God
Raven Simone Caples, May 2021

In the Shadows of God, Raven publicly and openly relives her journey through rejection, hurt, rape, negative self-image, sexual strongholds, and single motherhood, with the hope that other women will find strength in her transparency and faith in God.

Raven recounts numerous times in her life, from childhood to adulthood, when she persevered through devastation, homelessness, heartbreak, and interior and exterior struggles to arrive at the place of forgiveness, peace, and truth of God's unwavering love-the reality she lives in and shares with others today.

From being abandoned by her mother, to becoming her mother's end-of-life caregiver, Raven now recognizes God never abandoned her and she has never been outside the shadows of God.

Ladies First
Babette Bailey, May 2021

So many times, we feel like we've heard it all before; we've got it all together; we know what we're doing; we're equipped and ready; or like everybody is wrong, except us. We have even experienced times when we didn't want to hear another teaching, another preaching, another prophesy, or another video. We didn't want to read another book, another article, or another story. And we surely didn't want to talk about it anymore!

I want to encourage you to give it another try! Gather the women in your life, and let's embark on a continuous journey together to develop the Ladies First approach to life. ***Ladies First*** is a compilation of life experiences, Scriptural truths, and authentic thoughts on matters of the heart.

Demons Release Trilogies (Complete 3-Book Set)
Liberty Crouch, July 2021

- Am I going crazy?
- Was I born crazy?
- Was I groomed to be crazy?
- Or did you make me crazy?

These are honest questions that torment great people.

Explore the mind of a recovered addict, who wrestled with suicidal attempts, hallucinations, and extreme paranoia through free verse poetry, illustrations, authentic doctor reports, and journal entries.

Demons Release Trilogies, the complete 3-book series, enlightens each reader to the reality of demonic oppression, destructive consequences of suppressed neglect & abuse, and mistreated mental health challenges. The raw real-life testimony shared in these pages, is a compilation of decades of torment, followed by a great release.

Demons Release Trilogies reveal the ultimate Solution to every plaque, pain, abuse, and pitfall. You will be introduced to the One who came to seek and to save that which was lost and bind up the brokenhearted.

If you are suffering, have suffered, or love someone who is suffering with any of the above, this book is for you.

Gaining Strength for Your Journey
Diana Robinson, July 2021

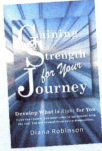

Gaining Strength for Your Journey will help you establish the necessary foundation to anchor your identity and equip you to make your dream a reality.

♦Have you done all you can to follow God's directions, only to be met with frustrating delays?

♦Have you ever wondered where God is when it seems like your destiny is deterred?

♦How will the life God designed for you actually become what you desire?

♦Will you remain diligent to rise to the level of distinction you were created for?

Gaining Strength for Your Journey will awaken the vision within you to operate confidently in all God has entrusted and packaged within you. The time is now to develop what is right for you.

God's Will, Will Be Done
Dedra Haynes-Waller, August 2021

Some losses were necessary! Whether we want to face it or not; the easy way or the hard way. In life, our will doesn't always line up with the will of God. So, we find ourselves going through life the hard way! God said, "Go right." We went left! God said, "Stand still and see the salvation of the Lord." We continue to *lay n play* in our mess. God said, "That's going to cost you if you do it that way." We say, "Let me see," knowing very well most of the time we can't afford the cost or the loss of that one thing He's trying to keep us from doing. Yet we allow our will to have its way! Read Romans 7:24-25.

The Power of Divine Partnership in Marriages
Teacher Oshowo, September 2021

God is the power source of every divinely ordained marriage. His intention is that each glorious marital destiny transcends to the next generation.

When the exemplary union between Christ and the church is not displayed through godly marriages, the world is in jeopardy.

Single, engaged, newlywed, or decades into the marriage, *The Power of Divine Partnership in Marriages* serves as a cornerstone guide to building a blissful future of unconditional love from the husband and unconditional submission from the wife.

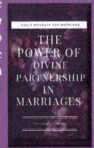

Experience a divinely distinct marriage today!
- Activate your spouse's role.
- Apply biblical practices.
- Leave a legacy of marriage done *right*!

Delilah the Distractor
T. Benton-Parker, September 2021

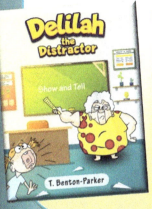

Distractions, distractions, distractions!

Use this upbeat story as a creative guide to help the children you love to:

- develop problem solving skills to remain focused in the classroom
- instill accountability
- raise awareness &
- be empathetic to classmates

Business Smart
Errol Beckford, October 2021

What separates a successful business from a failing one?

The success of your business depends on every move you make. Don't let the pandemic destroy your business. Make business work for you. Use this book as a blueprint to build the business of your dreams.

In *Business Smart*, you will learn:
- How to incorporate *The God Factor* into your business
- How to overcome *Fear of Failure*
- How to use *Business Smart* planning principles to achieve your goals

Glean from the success of pastor, author, business mentor, and entrepreneur Errol Beckford. Learn how he uses *The God Factor*, overcomes *Fear of Failure*, and applies *Business Smart* principles to transform his life and community.

When You Find the S.P.O.T.
Dedra Haynes-Waller, October 2021

Are you looking in the right places? Often times we are searching for something or a place that is right in front of our eyes. Literally, right in front of us!

We waste time, energy, and so much thought trying to possess something when God's word says, "But seek ye first the kingdom of God, and his righteousness; and all these things shall be added unto you" (Matthew 6:33 KJV).

In this book, *When You Find the S.P.O.T.*, five time author, Dedra Haynes-Waller, reveals how we can put all our trust and hope in man looking for a spot in the natural realm, when God has a supernatural S.P.O.T. picked out just for us!

Once we realize our place in Him and who we are, we will walk in the purpose we were created for. Remember, stop looking for validation from man and look for your S.P.O.T.

Demons Release Trilogies
The Prequel Book 3
Liberty Crouch, November 2021

The Prequel unveils the origin of the 3-part book series, ***Demons Release Trilogies***. It goes back to the beginning of the author's experiences during her recovery from lifelong drug addiction, mental health issues, and trauma. This authentic raw documentation contains excerpts from Liberty's ongoing journal entries, doctor reports, family history, and childhood. Tactics of the enemy to deter destiny are uncovered and the importance of identity, authority, and purpose are revealed.

This unique book is intentionally formatted to create interaction between the reader and the book itself. There are several opportunities for the reader to engage with the author's thoughts while coming to a deeper understanding of the free verse poetry and the doctors' reports. Through your personal reflection, the footsteps of your own journey will be revealed.

- ♦ Do you or someone you know desire to be mentally, emotionally, & spiritually free?
- ♦ Do you crave transformation for yourself or want to be able to effectively reach out to others who are hurting?

I Write What is Right!
Diana Robinson, December 2021

I Write What is Right reinforces daily positive affirmations from A-Z for children.

Say it!
Recognize it!
Read it!
Write it!
Meditate on it!
Believe it!
Be it!

I Write What is Right promotes letter & word recognition; handwriting, spelling, & reading practice; biblical values; and increased self-esteem.

Daily positive affirmations are key to clarity & confidence. You have the mind of Christ.

Proverbs 22:6
Train up a child in the way he should go, And when he is old he will not depart from it.

Poetic Inspirations
Babette Bailey, December 2021

Three-time author, Babette Bailey, authentically shares her heart in her newest book of poetry, *Poetic Inspirations*. You are guaranteed to find encouragement, laughter, reasons to celebrate, and good ol' fashion unapologetic advice within these pages. As you take a deep refreshing poetic breath, you will be inspired, renewed, and refreshed. There are tremendous amounts of love, strength, & positive wholesome messages in this book, heartfeltly prepared to be absorbed by women and men of all ages.

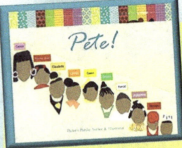

Pete!
Deloris Purdie, April 2022

Mama always said, "Time gon' tell who been doin' what."

Pete was the last born of ten children in the family. He learned as he entered middle school, that some labels are assigned according to the choices people continuously make. He realized, labels can be changed with just as much effort.

The labels of SLD (Specific Learning Disability) and mentally handicap that were assigned to Pete did not fit. He made a decision to do whatever was required to free himself. An encounter with a teacher that recognized his potential transformed his way of thinking, which in turn, changed the trajectory of Pete's life.

Heartbreak & Restoration: He Rescues Me
Imani Gillespie, April 2022

"Hurt does hurt. Emotional pain is devastating. Love is the very thing breathing air into our lungs. Love is maintaining the beat of our heart & connecting us to the beautiful things we partake in, in the world around us. We need Love to thrive. So, don't ever give up on Love."- Imani

♦ *Are you on a journey of healing & self-discovery?*

God can redeem anything and anyone. In the blurriness of pain, find purpose. Find liberty through honesty with yourself & God.

In **Heartbreak & Restoration**, you will take a journey inside Imani's heart as she learns how to become who God has created her to be, while struggling to be free in her mind from the life she's always led; the life she had been trained to accept.

I Write What is Right!
Diana Robinson, March 2022

Say it!
Recognize it!
Read it!
Write it!
Meditate on it!
Believe it!
Be it!

I Write What is Right! Cursive Edition reinforces daily positive affirmations for tweens & teens from A-Z.

Daily positive affirmations are key to clarity & confidence.

I Write What is Right! Cursive Edition establishes a Scriptural foundation to build self-esteem, resist bullying, and persevere through obstacles. You have the mind of Christ.

Proverbs 22:6
Train up a child in the way he should go,
And when he is old he will not depart from it.

My Alphabet Book
Colley A. Smith, May 2022

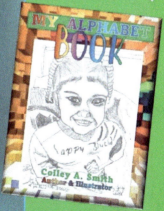

My Alphabet Book is interactive and ready to be personalized by the children you love.

Beautifully illustrated & engaging.

Created by a loving grandmother, Colley A. Smith, who made a quality decision in 2021 to share her God-given gifts of illustration and storytelling with the world.

All your children shall be taught by the Lord, and great shall be the peace of your children. -Isaiah 54:13

Come, Follow Me
Dynisha Warren-Fresneda, May 2022

Gain a fresh start. Find no greater love. Become separate & satisfied. Purge toxicity. Enjoy His presence. Build your relationship with God. Know you are blessed, even in a broken place. Purposefully surrender to God. Choose sacrificial worship. Beware of deception. Become a true worshipper. Stir up your gifts. Respond to Christ's invitation. Let's take a Christ-Centered journey together. *Come, Follow Me* is a life-enriching devotional journal, complete with relatable Bible-based teaching; guided writing tasks; & a planning section including monthly calendars and goal setting prompts.

Transformed through an intentional & intimate personal relationship with Jesus Christ herself, Dynisha compassionately challenges others to find what is right for them and proactively fulfill their God-given purpose.

CPSIA information can be obtained
at www.ICGtesting.com
Printed in the USA
BVHW010226060722
641423BV00007B/160